Half-Pint Pete
the Pirate

Sudipta Bardhan-Quallen

illustrated by

Geraldo Valério

G. P. Putnam's Sons
An Imprint of Penguin Group (USA) Inc.

G. P. PUTNAM'S SONS • A division of Penguin Young Readers Group.
Published by The Penguin Group.
Penguin Group (USA) Inc., 375 Hudson Street, New York, NY 10014, U.S.A.
Penguin Group (Canada), 90 Eglinton Avenue East, Suite 700, Toronto, Ontario M4P 2Y3, Canada
(a division of Pearson Penguin Canada Inc.).
Penguin Books Ltd, 80 Strand, London WC2R 0RL, England.
Penguin Ireland, 25 St. Stephen's Green, Dublin 2, Ireland (a division of Penguin Books Ltd.).
Penguin Group (Australia), 250 Camberwell Road, Camberwell, Victoria 3124, Australia
(a division of Pearson Australia Group Pty Ltd).
Penguin Books India Pvt Ltd, 11 Community Centre, Panchsheel Park, New Delhi - 110 017, India.
Penguin Group (NZ), 67 Apollo Drive, Rosedale, Auckland 0632, New Zealand (a division of Pearson New Zealand Ltd).
Penguin Books (South Africa) (Pty) Ltd, 24 Sturdee Avenue, Rosebank, Johannesburg 2196, South Africa.
Penguin Books Ltd, Registered Offices: 80 Strand, London WC2R 0RL, England.

Design by Annie Ericsson. Text set in Paradigm.
The art was done in acrylic on watercolor paper.
Library of Congress Cataloging-in-Publication Data
Bardhan-Quallen, Sudipta.
Half-Pint Pete the Pirate / Sudipta Bardhan-Quallen ; illustrated by Geraldo Valério.
p. cm.
Summary: Half-Pint Pete searches unsuccessfully for buried treasure
until he meets Belle, who has the other half of the map.
[1. Stories in rhyme. 2. Pirates—Fiction.]
I. Valério, Geraldo, 1970– ill. II. Title.
PZ8.3.B237Hal 2012 [E]—dc22 2011005691

ISBN 978-0-399-25173-3
1 3 5 7 9 10 8 6 4 2

To S,
who is complete all by herself
—S.B.-Q.

For Igor
—G.V.

Half-Pint Pete the Pirate
sailed half the seven seas.
He boarded half the ships he saw
and plundered them with ease.

Half his legs were made of pegs;
a patch hid half his eyes—
but with only half a treasure map,
he'd never found his prize.

"SAIL HO!" cried Pete one morning
as a far-off ship appeared.
"Let's pillage 'er, me mateys!"
His rowdy crewmates cheered.

He took the helm to chase the ship,
and then he had to laugh—
the other captain held aloft
an old map, torn in half.

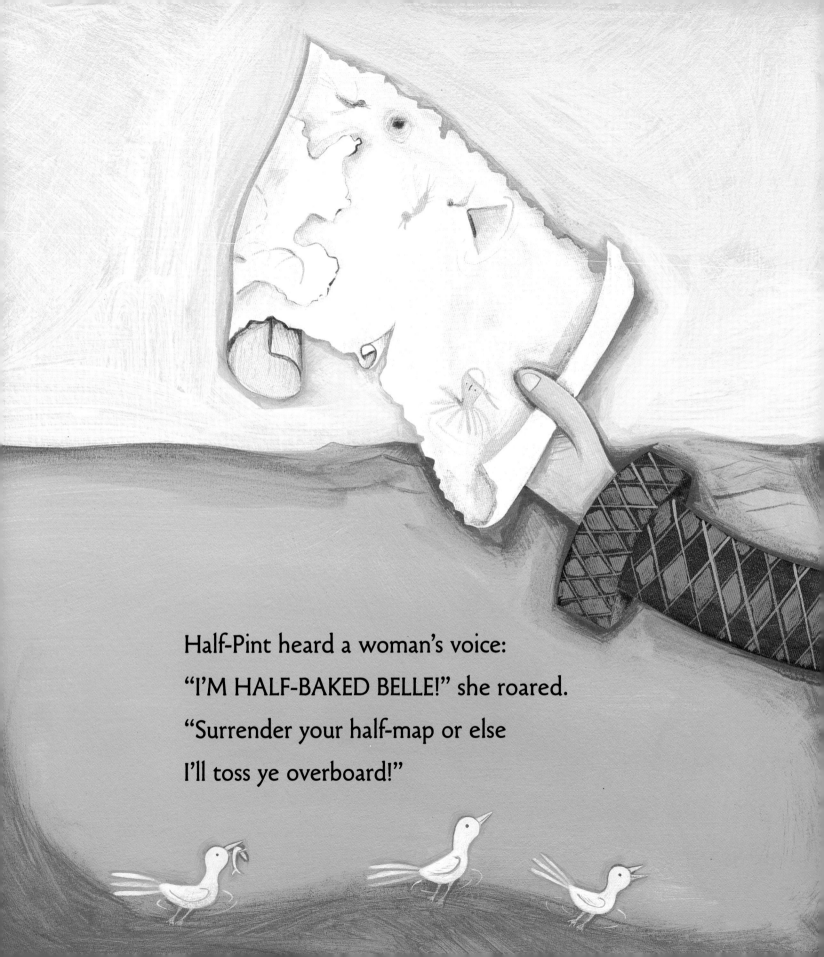

Half-Pint heard a woman's voice:
"I'M HALF-BAKED BELLE!" she roared.
"Surrender your half-map or else
I'll toss ye overboard!"

"Hold on," yelled Pete, "wait half a sec.

No need for us to fight.

The both of us are pirates.

We both want treasure, right?"

He held his half-map up to Belle's.
They were a perfect fit.

He said, "Let's both go halfsies.
Let's team up for a bit."

Aboard his ship, Pete told his crew,
"It's *Belle* we'll have to thank
when we find that long-lost gold . . .
and yet, she'll walk the plank!"

At last, they came upon the isle,
their final destination.
Pete grabbed a shovel and he said,
"Let's find the right location!"

He followed the directions,
but the spot he found was bare.
"This map is wrong, there's nothing here!"
he shouted in despair.

Half-Pint started blubbering;
Belle watched him with a frown.
She snatched the map and flipped it up.
"Ye fool! It's upside down!"

Belle pointed to a distant spot,
and there, without a doubt—
a halfway-open treasure chest
was sticking halfway out.

Belle hugged Pete and then he knew
he couldn't take her share.

Instead, Pete hugged her back and said,
"We make a perfect pair!"

Together, Pete and Belle began
to sail through every sea.
Pete swears they make the perfect two . . .

Except that, now, they're three!